Aberdeenshire
COUNCIL

Aberdeenshire Libraries
www.aberdeenshire.gov.uk/libraries

OCT 19

ABERDEENSHIRE
LIBRARIES
WITHDRAWN
FROM LIBRARY

D1493942

ABERDEENSHIRE
LIBRARIES
WITHDRAWN
FROM LIBRARY

Aberdeenshire

3228476

TITLES IN TWO SIDES:

GIRL NEXT DOOR

Karen Moncrieffe

SAM

Emma Norry

YOU DON'T CARE

Luisa Plaja

STOP

Jenni Spangler

LOOKING AFTER MUM

Roy Apps

BRUISED

Donna David

Badger Publishing Limited, Oldmedow Road, Hardwick Industrial Estate, King's Lynn PE30 4JJ

Telephone: 01438 791037

www.badgerlearning.co.uk

LOOKING AFTER MUM

ROY APPS

Looking After Mum ISBN 978-1-78837-325-8

Text © Roy Apps 2018
Complete work © Badger Publishing Limited 2018

All rights reserved. No part of this publication may be
reproduced, stored in any form or by any means mechanical,
electronic, recording or otherwise without the prior permission
of the publisher.

The right of Roy Apps to be identified as author of this
Work has been asserted by him in accordance with the Copyright,
Designs and Patents Act 1988.

Publisher: Susan Ross
Senior Editor: Danny Pearson
Editorial Coordinator: Claire Morgan
Copyeditor: Cheryl Lanyon
Designer: Bigtop Design Ltd
Cover Illustration: Dave Robbins

2 4 6 8 10 9 7 5 3 1

CHAPTER 1

DOUBLE CELEBRATION

Dani

Friday afternoon

I looked up at the clock on the classroom wall: 3.29pm.

I yawned. Still one minute to go until the end of school. But not just the end of school; the end of the week and the end of term, too.

It was tutor group. Ms Watson had already done the notices so we were just sitting there waiting. I started counting down the seconds. Ten, nine, eight...

At last the bell went. Everyone stuffed their books into their bags and made for the door.

I headed straight for the school gates.

"Dani!"

I spun round. Evie was racing towards me.

A word about Evie. I've known her since we were in nursery. She is my best mate. Not that we're very much alike. Evie is tall and sporty. Her dream is to go to the US and become a professional footballer. Me? I'm not tall. And I'm definitely not sporty. My thing is singing. School talent contests, karaoke, in the shower — basically, I'll sing anywhere. Evie says it's because I like the sound of my own voice. She's allowed to say that because she's my best mate.

"Have you seen the boys?" Evie asked.

"No," I replied.

Evie and I were meant to be meeting up with

Matt, Bradley and Mo. After a bit, I saw Bradley and Mo walking slowly towards us. Honestly, I've seen snails move faster.

"Come on!" I yelled.

Slowly they caught us up.

"Where's Matt?" I asked.

"Where do you think? Bunking off school," muttered Mo. "Again."

"Well, it is his birthday," Evie pointed out.

"He's been missing loads of lessons lately," said Bradley. "He's well behind with his Design Tech project."

"He didn't show up for the match on Wednesday afternoon either," Mo added. "They had to put some Year 9 kid in goal. We lost 6–0. It was embarrassing."

I frowned. "That doesn't sound like Matt," I said.

"Coach said he'd be out of the team if he pulled that kind of stunt again," said Mo.

"He'd better turn up tonight," said Bradley.

Matt's mum was paying for us all to have a meal at Simply Pizza to celebrate his birthday and, as it was also the last day of term, it was a kind of double celebration.

"Of course he'll show up," I said. "Missing school or a football match is one thing, but nobody misses their own birthday celebrations."

Evie and I left the boys to get their bus. They live at the other end of town from us.

"It should be a really good evening," Evie said. "Especially for you."

"What do you mean, especially for me?"

"Honestly Dani, sometimes you're just so thick. He likes you."

"Don't be stupid," I said, hoping my face hadn't turned bright pink.

Deep down, though, I was quite excited. I decided to make a special effort getting ready for Matt's birthday meal.

CHAPTER 2

BLIND PANIC

Matt

Friday morning

I looked at the letter again.

Dear Ms Edwards

Matthew's attendance at school continues to be unsatisfactory. I would be grateful if you would telephone the school as soon as possible to make an appointment to discuss this matter.

Yours sincerely,

M Khan

Head of Student Performance KS4

Luckily, I'd got to the post before Mum. I'd seen the school crest on the envelope and had guessed what it was. There was no way I wanted her to see it. It would only worry her. She knew how much school I was missing. I put the letter in a drawer. At least, with it being the Easter holidays, I could forget about it for a couple of weeks.

I had actually planned on going into school today. As well as catching up on my work, I wanted to remind the others about my birthday meal at Simply Pizza. But when I'd looked in on Mum first thing, I knew it would mean another full day at home.

A couple of months ago my mum had a stroke. A stroke happens when the blood supply to your brain is cut off for a while. It's like a brain attack. Now she finds all sorts of everyday stuff difficult: walking, getting out of bed, even holding a knife and fork — one of her hands doesn't work properly. Her face is a bit lop-sided and sometimes she slurs her words a little. She has physiotherapy but she still needs a lot of help.

"Matt," she'd told me when she first came out of hospital, "there's no knowing how I'm going to feel from one day to the next. There will be bad days, but there will also be better days."

Today was a bad day. I had to help her out of bed and along the hall to the toilet.

She took ages getting dressed. When she eventually came through to the kitchen, she still hadn't managed to do up the buttons on her cardigan.

"Fancy some breakfast, Mum?" I asked, once I'd helped her get her cardigan on properly.

She nodded. "But you get on, you'll be late for school."

I shook my head. "Teacher training day," I lied. By the time I'd cleared away the breakfast things, put the washing on and sorted out her lunch, there wouldn't have been much point in going to school anyway.

"You'll have plenty of time to get ready for this evening then," Mum replied. It had been her idea to pay for a meal out for me and some of my mates as a birthday present. "Who have you invited?"

"Mo and Bradley."

Mum frowned. "Mo and Bradley? Have I met them?" Mum is always nosy about who I hang out with.

"No, I've only got to know them this term. They're in the same Design Tech class as me."

"So, just the three of you then?"

"No, there's a couple of girls, too. Evie and Dani."

I was on safer ground here, I knew. Mum had met Evie and Dani. They had popped in once when Evie's dad was giving us a lift to a footie tournament. Evie was captaining the girls' first eleven, I was in goal for the under sixteens and

Dani… well, I think she just came along for the ride. I knew Mum thought that they were both 'nice girls'.

She grinned one of her slightly lop-sided grins. "Oh yes, I remember. A tall, sporty girl and her little friend who's a bit of a chatterbox," she said, raising her eyebrow in a really annoying way.

I sighed. "Mum, we're just mates, that's all."

"Yes, of course, dear."

*

Friday early evening

Mum began to feel better as the day went on. I made her scrambled eggs for dinner and then I messaged Dani to let her know I'd see them all at Simply Pizza at about seven. None of my mates knows about Mum's stroke. How could I possibly tell them? Explain what it had done to her; what life is like now?

I was in the bathroom, busy getting to work with the hair wax, when I heard a loud crash from the kitchen.

I charged downstairs. Mum was lying on the kitchen floor surrounded by broken plates. Her eyes were full of tears.

"Mum?"

Suddenly, her whole body shook and she started sobbing. Great, big, terrifying howls. "Look at me! I'm useless! Completely useless! Sometimes I wish I was dead!"

"Mum!" I yelled, blind panic filling every part of me. "Don't say things like that!"

I sat down on the floor beside her and waited for the tears to stop.

CHAPTER 3

BLUSHING ALL OVER

Dani

Friday evening

I called round for Evie. As soon as she opened the door she gave me a long, hard look.

"Nice," she said. "You have been busy."

"What do you mean?" I asked, although I knew very well what she was on about.

"Your lippy for a start," Evie replied.

I shrugged. "So… what's wrong with it?"

"Nothing! It's just that I'm not used to seeing you wearing lipstick."

She was right, of course. I didn't usually wear lipstick. In fact, I didn't actually own any lipstick. I'd borrowed it from my sister. Or, to be more accurate, I'd stolen it from my sister.

Evie gave me a sly wink. "Keen to try and impress a certain boy, are we?"

I ignored her.

"I hope it's worth it," Evie went on. "You know what these boys are like. Most of the time they don't notice anything."

When we got to Simply Pizza, Bradley and Mo were already there. They'd found us a really nice table in the corner. The last time I ate here, it was with my sister and we were right next to the loo. Gross!

"Matt not here yet?" I asked.

"I'll check, shall I?" replied Mo. He bent down and made a point of looking under the table. "No, he doesn't seem to be here," he said, with a laugh.

"He probably missed the bus," said Bradley.

The waitress came over to take our order. Straightaway, I recognised her from school. She was one of the Year 12 prefects. According to her name badge she was called Martha.

"Are you ready to order yet?" she asked, with a pout.

"We're still waiting for someone," I explained, wondering where on earth Matt had got to.

Martha sighed and rolled her eyes. "Look. We're really busy tonight so if you're not going to order, we're going to have to ask you to give up the table for another group."

"We'd better order," said Mo. "We can order for Matt, too."

"Good idea," Evie agreed, "I'm starving."

We ordered our pizzas, plus an extra one for Matt.

Evie looked at her watch and frowned. "Where is he? Has he texted or anything?"

"I haven't heard from him," said Bradley.

"Me neither," added Mo.

Evie shot me a look. I must have been blushing. "Well, Dani?" she asked.

"He texted me earlier," I replied. "He said 'see you there'."

"Ring him," said Evie.

I rang Matt. It went straight to voicemail. I looked up and saw everyone staring at me.

"Well, go on!" hissed Evie. "Leave a message!"

"Er… hi Matt," I said. Everybody's eyes were on me. "Yeah… er… we're all at Simply Pizza? We're wondering where you are. Hope you're OK?"

I put my phone down on the table. I stared at it, willing it to ring, but it stayed silent.

Martha came with our orders. "Enjoy," she said.

Everyone else started eating, but I'd lost my appetite. Where was Matt? Something must have happened. But what?

As the others continued to stuff their faces, I texted Matt again. Twice. I didn't get a reply either time.

Bradley turned to me. "He's not going to show, is he?"

"Doesn't look like it," I shrugged.

Bradley grabbed Matt's pizza and shared it with Mo.

By the time everyone had finished eating, there was still no sign of Matt. Martha came over with the bill. It came to just under £60.

"Looks like we're going to have to settle the bill ourselves," sighed Mo. "£15 each."

Everyone groaned.

Martha was hovering over us. "Is there a problem?" she asked, with an annoying smile.

"It's just that we were expecting our mate to pay, but he hasn't turned up," explained Mo.

"Oh dear," Martha sighed. "I'll just call over the manager."

"We can pay!" Evie snapped. "All right?"

Mo lent Bradley some cash. Evie found she had just enough in her purse, too. All I had was my emergency ten-pound note and five pound coins, which would have been plenty for my bus fare home, but I'd have to use them all to pay the bill.

"Looks like you'll have to walk home," said Mo.

"You could give your dad a ring. Ask him to pick you up," Evie said to me. She grinned. "You can give me a lift!"

The boys waited with us outside. Dad finally appeared. Of course, he had to introduce himself to everyone. "Hi guys!" he said, with a stupid smile on his face. "I'm Roger, Dani's father! Have you all had a good time?"

Talk about cringeworthy. I was so embarrassed. I knew my face was bright red.

I was totally miserable. And it was all Matt's fault. I couldn't believe that I'd actually thought he was an OK kind of guy! Who doesn't turn up to their own birthday party? How rude! Couldn't he have messaged me at least to say he was OK? That he wasn't coming?

CHAPTER 4
LYING AGAIN

Matt

Friday evening

Once Mum had managed to stop crying, I helped her up off the floor. We sat down at the kitchen table.

"I'm sorry, Matt. I didn't mean what I just said. About wishing I was dead. It's just that everything's so frustrating."

"Don't worry, Mum," I told her. "Like I've said before, I'll look after us."

Mum sighed. "But Matt, it's not fair on you.

Apart from anything else, you've been missing school."

I thought about the letter hidden in my desk upstairs.

"Oh, that's not a problem. They know I have to take time out to help you," I lied.

The fact was, there was no one else to look after Mum. When she had her stroke, they took her to hospital. My Gran came to stay and looked after us for a bit, but then she had to go back to Spain where she lives with her new partner.

She told us she'd try and get over to the UK again soon, but she hasn't yet.

Mum does have a physiotherapist come to visit her. But he doesn't do the cooking and the washing and ironing and stuff. That's not his job.

"I keep trying to do things and then find I can't," Mum said. "That's how I ended up on the kitchen floor. Because I was feeling a bit better,

I thought I'd try and wash up the plates. But I dropped the lot and when I tried to pick it all up I fell over."

Mum grabbed my hand in her good hand and held it tight. We sat there for a moment like that.

I heard my phone ringing upstairs.

"That will be your friends," said Mum. "You should go or else you'll be late for your birthday meal."

I shook my head. "I'm not going."

"But you can't let them down, love. Look, I'll still be here when you get back."

I shook my head. "I'll stay here with you."

Mum sighed. "Well, you'd better message them to let them know."

"OK," I said. "But first I'll help you through to the sitting room so you can watch the TV."

Once Mum was settled, I went back to the kitchen, cleared up the mess on the floor and put the kettle on. Whenever Mum had a fall, she'd get a bit wobbly on her legs. I knew I'd have to help her up the stairs to bed later.

I took her a cup of tea. She forced a weak smile. "What did your friends say?" she asked.

"Oh, they were fine with it," I lied. "We're going to do it another time."

Of course I hadn't messaged them. How could I? What would I say?

Oh, hi guys! Sorry, you'll have to buy your own pizzas tonight, only I'm busy looking after my mum. Yeah… she had a stroke, right? Keeps falling over. Can't even hold a cup properly. Yeah, and sometimes she wishes she was dead!

I liked my mates and I liked Dani especially — not that the others knew that. But how could I ever begin to explain to Dani, or any of them, what I was feeling? Why I had let them all down?

*

Early Saturday morning

It was early when I woke up the next morning.
I lay there for ages, not really wanting to get up.

I decided to check my phone. There was a
voicemail message and a couple of texts, all from
Dani. I'd have to text her back, I thought, but
what could I say? Well, I'd lied once, telling Mum
I'd let my mates know I wouldn't be coming to
Simply Pizza. And I'd lied telling her there was
no problem with the school.

There was nothing else for it: I'd just have to lie
again.

CHAPTER 5

FROZEN WITH FEAR

Dani

Saturday morning

Evie and I met up in the shopping centre. We were going to look around the clothes shops.

"Have you heard anything from Matt yet?" she asked.

I nodded. "Yeah, he texted me this morning." I let her read the text on my phone.

Sorry I didn't make it. I'm in bed with a really bad cold.

Evie frowned. "A really bad cold? That came on a bit suddenly, didn't it? I mean, you said he texted you yesterday to say he'd see us there."

I shrugged. "I suppose colds can come on very quickly," I said. But I knew how weak it sounded even before I'd finished speaking.

"He's making excuses," Evie said. "He let us down badly last night and he doesn't want to tell us why." It did seem the most likely explanation. What could have happened? Had he found someone better to celebrate with at the last minute? How had I got Matt so wrong?

"I'd still like to know the real reason he didn't show up last night," I muttered.

Evie grabbed my arm. "Come on," she said, "he's not worth getting upset about. Let's go to Bubbles. I'll buy you a hot chocolate."

We'd started to make our way to Bubbles when Evie stopped suddenly and pulled me back. "Look!" she hissed. "Coming out of the supermarket. Isn't that Matt?"

"You're right, it is! In bed with a really bad cold?

Who does he think he's kidding?" I was furious. "Matt!" I yelled.

Matt spun round and saw us. He started to run.

"Matt!" I shouted. "Come back!"

He carried on running. Evie and I chased after him. We ran right through the shopping centre. Evie was way out in front of me.

We'd reached the High Street when Matt turned round and saw Evie gaining on him. Blindly, he jumped off the pavement and into the road. I was quite far behind Evie, but I could still see what was about to happen.

I wanted to shout out to warn him, but I was frozen with fear.

He didn't see the bus coming. There was an angry blast of a horn and a sickening screech of brakes as it headed straight for him.

CHAPTER 6

FRIENDS

Matt

Saturday afternoon

I was dead tired and not thinking straight, that was the trouble. Not only that, I was really desperate to avoid Dani and Evie. I didn't want to have to try and explain to them just what was going on in my life.

Before I knew it, the bus was bearing down on me, the driver sounding his horn like a madman. I threw myself out of its path and felt the whoosh of its slipstream just as I managed to roll onto the pavement on the other side of the road.

When I struggled up off the ground, people were staring at me like I was some drug-crazed junkie. The traffic was still rushing by; Evie and Dani would have to wait a while to cross the road. I raced off. Luckily, not too much of the shopping had been squashed when I landed on the pavement.

Mum was asleep in front of the TV when I got back home. I left the fish pieces and baked beans out for dinner and put the rest of the shopping away.

I had an hour or so free before I had to start cooking dinner. I should have got started on some coursework, I knew, but I was so tired and there was so much of it: I just couldn't face it.

*

Sunday afternoon

It was about tea-time when I heard the doorbell.

"I'll go," I called out.

When I reached the hall, I froze. Through the window at the side of the front door I could see the whole crowd of them: Dani, Evie, Mo and Bradley. I knew why they were here. They wanted to find out why I had let them down; why I'd lied to them about having a cold. I stepped back away from the door.

"Matt?" I turned round and saw Mum standing there. She'd made it through to the hall using her walking stick.

"Aren't you going to let them in?" she asked.

I shook my head. "No way!"

Mum sighed. She put her good hand on the door handle.

"No, Mum, please! I don't want to see them!"

"Well, I do," Mum said. "After all, it was me who invited them to come round."

"You what?"

Before I could stop her she had opened the door.
The four of them were there, loaded down with
bags.

"Dani! Evie! How nice to see you again!" cried
Mum. "And you two lads must be Mo and
Bradley. Come on through."

Dani fixed me with a big grin. "Hi, Matt! Happy
birthday!"

Mo clapped me on the back. "How goes it,
mate?"

"If I could just take your arm, Evie," said Mum.
She took Evie's arm and the others followed
them into the sitting room. I stood there in the
hall, speechless, until I came to my senses and
went through after them.

Dani was still grinning. "I'll explain, shall I?"

"That would be a good idea, Dani," agreed

Mum, giving her a wink. "I've kept my promise. I haven't told Matt anything."

"We were all worried about you when you didn't show up on Friday…" Dani began.

I caught Mo and Bradley nodding in agreement.

"… and I didn't believe for one moment that you'd suddenly gone down with a bad cold…"

Mum frowned and cast me a sideways look.

"… so, after Evie and I saw you in the shopping centre, I decided to find out just what was going on with you. I rang your mum. She told me everything."

I glanced at Mum. "Including about my stroke," she said. "And about how you've had to help look after me."

"Then your mum had this brilliant idea," Dani went on. "As you had missed your birthday meal at Simply Pizza, why didn't we all have a surprise party for you here?"

She turned to Mo, Bradley and Evie. "Come on guys, let's show him what we've brought."

Out of their bags came a whole load of Indian takeaway: chicken tikka, onion bhajees, samosas, naan bread, the lot.

While Evie, Mo and Bradley sorted out the food, I went through to the kitchen to get some plates and knives and forks. Dani followed me through. "I'm so sorry about your mum," she said. She paused and suddenly looked serious. "I know about strokes."

"Yeah?"

Dani nodded. "Yeah. My grandad had one."

"Oh... I see..." I took a deep breath. "Look, I'm really sorry about Friday night. It's just... Mum had a fall and... then..." I couldn't think what to say.

Dani put a hand on my shoulder. "You don't need to try and explain," she said. "I'll be here for you Matt. Whatever."

There was a lump in my throat. "Thanks, Dani," I managed to whisper.

Dani pulled a face. "But don't expect me to swap my Music Tech option for Design Tech just so I can sit next to you in class!"

I grinned. "What a terrifying thought!"

"Come on," Dani said, smiling and taking my hand. "There's a chicken tikka in there with your name on it."

We all started to eat. Dani gave Mum a hand with her curry. I looked round the room at them all. As Mum had said, there would be bad days and better days. Today was definitely a better day.

Of course, it wouldn't cure my mum's stroke, or the worry and pain that might come with it, but one thing I now knew for certain: when it came to looking after Mum, I wouldn't be alone. No, I had friends — really good friends — who would be there for me.

Young Carers

What is a Young Carer?

A Young Carer is someone under the age of 18 who helps look after someone in their family who is ill, or who helps by looking after the rest of the family while the sick person can't.

How many people are Young Carers?

It's estimated that there are around 700,000* Young Carers in the UK. That's about one out of every twelve secondary-school-age students.

What do Young Carers do?

Young Carers find themselves with more responsibilities than other young people. They are likely to have to do more household chores than is usual. They may also provide emotional support to the person they are caring for; or learn how to nurse them or look after their personal needs, like bathing and dressing.

*2017 figures

What kind of problems do Young Carers face?

Young Carers often have less free time than other young people. Sometimes their friends don't understand this. It can be stressful, worrying and tiring being a Young Carer, too. They may find that they have less time to themselves, or to do their homework. Sometimes, it can be hard to concentrate at school.

The Carers Trust

The Carers Trust offers help and advice for Young Carers. They also organise an annual Young Carers Awareness Day.

You can visit their website:

www.carers.org/about-us/about-young-carers

Or contact them at:

Info@carers.org

ABOUT THE AUTHOR

Roy Apps is the author of over 90 books for children and young adults. He has also written for lots of television programmes.

He lives in the country near Hastings with his wife and grown-up son. They have ten rare-breed sheep, fifteen chickens, five ducks, three cats and a dog.

Roy is passionate about music and, when he's not writing, he likes to pretend that he's an incredible jazz pianist.

He enjoys gardening and supports Brighton & Hove Albion Football Club. He gets his best ideas when he's walking his dog, Holly.